Sleep Cinematic or A Golem's Quartet

Published by Gnashing Teeth Publishing. All rights reserved.

Original Cover Art by Lim "Wave" Zinyee.

The font used is Candara.

The cover font is Albhadi.

Editor-in-Chief Karen Cline-Tardiff

Assistant Editor Jennifer Taylor

Printed in the United States of America

ISBN 979-8-9854833-0-7

Fiction: Poetry

Sleep Cinematic or A Golem's Quartet

Poems of Chats and River Boat Trips

Ideas Inside

I

A Golem stumbles into a synagogue
And begs the Rabbi for a touch of clay.
"Can you sculpt a better shape for my nose?
Change this face, give me a Bogie gaze?"
So pleaded the Golem.
"My! You would be handsome, quite fetching,"
Said the Rabbi.
"Perhaps a third nostril, or a dramatic bridge.
That should stop the innocent from retching."

II

The Rabbi stood firm before the Golem
And fussed with the earth creature's flashy hair.
"Be sure to wear your Kippah while in our house.
Be duly observant otherwise the cantor will stare."
So whispered the Rabbi.
"A skullcap I lovingly wear, but what of my broken nose?"
Whined the Golem.
"A dramatic bridge seems gaudy, perhaps too gripping.
While at it, can you fix my eight cumbersome toes?"

III

The Golem tripped over the Bimah steps
And glimmered under The Everlasting Light.
"I need my nose set straight, to start me anew.
Find home in this land, edge everything to right."
So confessed the Golem.
"You were made to shock, sculpted to guard,"
Replied the Rabbi.

"Step away from the holy light, return your Kippah.
Go to the street, but don't take such news too hard."

IV

The Golem raised a finger to clean his nose.
And swirled out a good day's worth of debris.
"Crushed noses… so hard to clean, keep pristine.
My finger's plucked rocks, I've that muck and bleed."
So uttered the Golem.
 "This here is my essence, this terracotta nugget,"
Added the Golem.
"How about a tissue for my tears, not my snot,
How I wish to wear righteous garb, Tefilin and Tallit."

V

The Eternal Light glowed above the howling Golem,
And he begged the Rabbi's permission to stay.
"But I've jowls, revered Rabbi, jiggling jowls.
And see how my eight toes achingly splay."
So argued the Golem.
"There you have it, such oddly shaped essence,"
Returned the Rabbi.
"You must leave! Stumble to the way you came.
It is not for you to stand in God's presence."

VI

Slumping shoulders, the Golem stepped away from the Light
And considered another point to fit his need.
"I've got paunch, drooping and dusting all floors.
And I've got wrinkles from an exacting age I concede."
So insisted the Golem.
"Like children, I can gulp, put out candles with one blow,"
Continued the Golem.
"Then from another end, like all living souls,
I can blast one long solemn Golem wind concerto."

VII

The Golem gazed lovingly upon the tall Ark.
And he heaved a sigh; he no longer felt emboldened.
"Was it not from an imagination within here
That I was fashioned, to guard here thus molded?"
So asked the Golem.
"All of that is true, true as your heart of clay,"
Said the Rabbi.
"You have our gratitude, our deepest admiration.
Best to close shop and clock out for the day."

XIII

The Rabbi led the troubled Golem to the door
And placed a caring hand on his slumped shoulder.
"There's ugliness waiting just past our thatched Sukkah,
Such ugliness, which make us dogged, all the more bolder."
So reflected the Rabbi.
"We should all celebrate, a festival joyous and fertile,"
Continued the Rabbi.
"Watch over us as we weave Lulav and hang the right fruit.
Shield us while we pray amongst willow and myrtle."

IX

The Golem stepped outside the synagogue.
And felt atop for a sliding prayer cap.
"How did I do it, how could I not know,
I've become a golem thief? Guilt becomes my trap."
So shrieked the Golem.
"Here comes the storm, it's ready to pour,"
Said the Rabbi.
"Keep the Kippah. Wear it in observance.
Now go on! Go on home! I need close and lock the door."

X

A wounded Golem waddled home in the storm
And thought of an evening in the barber's chair.
"Perhaps a mountainous quiff or a wavy pompadour,
Even a Golem's Bun, the exact style for a Golem's hair."
So mused the Golem.
"As for days like these, there's too much to give strain,"
Mused the Golem more.
"Worry stifles limb and loin and shutters the gut;
We Golems tend to lose weight in such an autumn rain."

XI

His Golem belly melted off into a neighboring sewer
And he watched his essence drift towards the great Ohio.
"I'm told I'm shaped from the Scioto's finest mud,
A belittled child from the grandest American Rio."
So thought the Golem.
"Hands in the air! Pass over all cash you carry as habit,"
Shouted a mangy mugger.
"Hand over each penny and dime.
As God as your witness! You're being robbed by a Rabbit!"

XII

A Bandit Hare blocked the Golem's path
And held up the oppressed with a stern paw.
"I've not much in possession, save this prayer cap.
But I might lend a good listening ear if you've a saw."
So suggested the Golem.
"No cash but flesh? I may just wish to bend your ear,"
Said the Marauding Bunny.
"This street's quite gloomy, a rough place to live.
Whenever I speak of my troubles, rabbits mostly sneer."

The Golem plucked off his right ear
And handed it off to the reflective thief.
"I need only one ear to keep steady my new Kippah,
Maintain a devout poise and reject grief."
So conjectured the Golem.
"Keep your ear and your Kippah feeling,"
Said the Hare.
"I've a better thought, a dire need.
Please lead me towards cover, a loving ceiling."

XIV

The Golem led the Hare to his humble home
And for cover under his favorite alley awning.
"Here is where we can stay,
It's a cozy Golem lodge, ripe for yawning."
So said the exhausted Golem.
"To hover safely grip this here knurl,"
Added one friend to another.
"See all the people walk by a Golem and a Hare,
I love this Here; from this Here I took my name – Pearl."

XV

The Hare returned the detached lobe and company
And gave his friend a discerning frown.
"Pearl! I'd hardly call you a skilled surgeon.
You've gone and hung your right ear upside down."
So shouted the bemused Hare.
"It's just as well! It's a protective way to be,"
Said the Golem.
"Ears are misdirected; they never bend for comfort.
I need radar just what might be catching up to me."

I

The Golem stumbled about Pearlie Alley with guilt rising.
And stomped to pieces a poor mouse's tail.
"I am a skullcap crook, a lowly Kippah bandit!
As sure as I am here, I am off on a swindler's trail."
So moaned the Golem to the Hare.
"I stepped into a shul for a moment's reverence,"
Continued the teary-eyed creature.
"I walked right out with a Kippah, another's Kippah,
As if it were my own, my spiritual severance."

II

The Hare hopped about into the Pearlie Alley
And swiftly kicked the Golem's protruding posterior.
"Never mind the stealing of that heady top.
You stepped on the blameless, one much littler."
So admonished the Hare.
 "I hear tears on tin somewhere in this alley near,"
Said the Golem.
"I am clumsy, I confess. I step by thunder,
Yet, I hear them from my backwards, my upside-down ear."

III

The Golem and Hare followed the sound of tears on tin
And found a mouse locked tight within a trap.
"Someone crushed my tail, sending me into this cell.
Now my tail's twisted and turned, a trapezoidal chap."
So said the Mouse.
"So sorry minute mouse, beware my clumsy fat feet,"
Apologized the Golem.

"Your tail is much like my toes, twisted and turned.
But such is the fate of the scrawny, the exposed petite."

IV

The mouse then studied cheese lying in the trap
And hoped for the best of crumbs.
"I shall sing 'O Sole Mio' in this steel box.
I will sing it in my original mousy Italian hum."
So bragged the mouse.
"Winter foraging proves weak, I've looked in the weeds,"
Sighed the mouse.
"My tastes are simple, though my name is Fred.
Havarti! How about excellent sesame seeds?"

V

Fred thought lovingly of a favorite soprano opera star,
And dreamed of her ever and after in his oblong cellblock.
"She pleasures my pulse when she sings 'Un bel di'.
She shall be the butterfly of my every day, round the clock."
So fawned Fred.
"We'll be covered by a flower flood, a cherry blossoms squall,"
Said the mouse.
"I've got food and I've got whimsy.
Think how fancy those soft cherry blossoms shall fall."

VI

Fred pooped about the steel mousetrap
And settled in for a show, as if he were at the Mariinsky.
"Bring on the Snow Ladies! Bring on singing anvils clinking.
Perhaps a comic Hamlet, or a tragic Agatha Christie."
So hooted Fred.
"I will shriek 'Brava, Bravi,' a one-mousy claque,"
Chuckled Fred.
"I've the ears! I've a giant's heart!
My cheers shall be flashy, but with the usual rodent tack."

VII

The Golem ran his fingers across trap's skylight ceiling
And introduced himself along with the Hare, Jarry.
"I have ears that reach past and future directions.
Tell me; which cantor sings better tropes, Hamlet or Havarti?"
So questioned the Golem.
"The song's the thing, with notes better when brighter,"
Professed the Mouse.
"Then both are raucous tunes, tummy delights.
Though, one must admit, Havarti ages much finer."

VIII

The Mouse ran the length of the trap, end to end,
And the Golem followed with a muscular index finger.
"At which end might I find her, my beloved Soprano Star?
At which can I find that lovely Coloratura Singer."
So wondered the Mouse.
"I have to cut you with truth, facts for those in fur,"
Interjected Jarry.
"Sopranos rarely sing for us! Some prefer to eat or even fear us.
Still, hold fondness for her when you sleep cinematic; it's a shattered heart cure."

IX

Indeed! No soprano walked into Fred's trap to sing.
And calm took over as Fred stood amongst his poop.
"She's never been a butterfly, Oh Jo! Oh Jo!"
I'm here alone and she's off with her opera troupe."
So realized the Mouse.
"She's beyond my reach, distant, despite my swoon,"
Mourned the Mouse.
"Still, she's in this world! She's in this world!
She's my kind Queen of my Night, perched on a half moon."

Fred peered upwards, searching for a Soprano on a Half Moon,
And hummed 'O Sole Mio' quickly, just the refrain.
"I seek the Soprano on the Half-moon. My Joy! My Joy!
But only see darkness, no matter how I strain."
So wailed the Mouse.
"Malicious Clouds block the view, like a massive clay wall,"
Said the Mouse.
"But I would like to join the Golem, dance with the Hare.
So, I shall howl, make a furious cry straight from this stall."

XI

The Golem removed his hand from the trap's top
And sunlight heated the tin snare's floors.
"Let's free the Mouse, invite him to a song.
There's a palace nearby, coloraturas within its doors."
So shared Jarry.
"Crush the box, Pearl, set loose Mr. Fred,"
Suggested the Hare.
"Free the fellow, and we'll hop over to that palace.
We'll help him find his home, his operatic cred."

XII

The Mouse tucked into a corner
And waited for the Golem to pulverize the tin.
"Monsieur Jarry, how is that you are so kind?
To become such a saint, a bunny without sin?"
So asked the relieved Mouse.
"Oh, I can hardly be credited as such, friend in snare,"
Returned the Rabbit.
"It's a childhood tragedy, a nightmarish memory
That explains how I became a Highway Hare."

The Golem carefully peeled away the top of the trap
And from his prison Fred made a crouch and spring.
"As if it were yesterday, Oh such a tremendous loss.
Cozy nest, first summer, munching on turnip greens."
So reflected Jarry.
"When we heard grinding, clang and roar,"
Mused the Rabbit.
"A swirling blade, slashing grass into a ghastly manicure.
As God reads baseball scores in heaven, my poor Mother's head it tore."

XIV

The Golem and Fred heard this tale with horror
And quivered at the thought of losing a mother.
"Swishing blades blew twister winds throughout our nest,
With one big hack I lost yet another."
So spoke Jarry.
"What he lost hangs on a key chain some allege,"
Said the Rabbit.
"Those blades lashed away my brother's foot.
So, as a craft Highway Hare I seek revenge."

XV

The Golem and the Mouse stood mesmerized by the Rabbit's grit
And leaned in to capture Jarry's every word.
"I took to the old 3-C Road to terrorize those hiding in shrubs
I mugged every creature, every dog, ferret and bird."
So growled the bunny.
"How… From how many did you take money?"
Queried the Golem.
"You were the first! And even there I took not a penny.
I ask you, friends, be fair; who cries for the suffering bunny?"

Book 1
Scene 3
Ghost Light Trio

I

Pearl, Fred, and Jarry darted towards the opera palace
And passed a shop with papers from Warsaw to Montreal.
"I love a good exposition, shows with pools of laughter.
I suspect Fred's soprano star's warbles are amongst the best of all."
So noted Jarry.
"It is the blasting of the Shofar that I long to hear,"
Interrupted the Golem.
"Its timbre and tune rams way into my clay core.
With every New Year, I hop and boogie. It makes me shake my rear. "

II

The Golem, Mouse and Hare scampered under a half moon
And thinning clouds opened for a dim lunar glow.
"She sings with brilliance, a delight in every way.
I fancy her a Teatro star, even a rainbow in Guangzhou."
So gabbed the Mouse.
"I cannot only imagine the life within the opera palace stage door,"
Jabbered the worldly opera mouse.
"Puffy bassos and delicate tenors, haughty altos and Distraught Divas!
Oh, and spectacular tale, funny triangular tales, and more and more and
more."

III

The Golem smashed into a trashcan, rearranging his nose,
And took beatific flip into signage barking no parking zone.
"The marvelous thing about creatures made up of clay,
Is that we can crash shapely and call that new shape our own."
So said the dauntless Golem.
"I've tripped over cans along the shores my muddy birth river,"
Boasted the Golem.

"And rolled from Broad to Main to the Rich Street Bridge.
Come now, Fred and Hare, there's no need for worry or quiver."

IV

Fred, pointing at the stage door, pressed his face against its wall
And ran his whiskers searching for a place to slip in.
"With some minor twisting, I can slip through any jamb.
I'll slide my... oof... paw, flatten my... oof... belly, pull my... oof... chin."
So grunted the Mouse.
"Now that you are in, plant your paws, find your balance,"
Coached the Hare.
"Give the door a heave so that once we're all in,
We'll find your beloved soprano in this old movie palace."

V

Fred made his way through the jamb, except for his tail,
And hung before the palace house, every box and chair.
"I believe I am stuck and thumping against wall like a clanging bell.
I hear you all laughing, each everyone, both Pearl and Mr. Hare."
So rang Fred.
"Be ready, Fred, and I'll give the door a heave with one broad shoulder,"
Announced Pearl.
"Make it quick, Pearl, for I think I can see her, my soprano star.
What I should say to her, oh sue me, someone, to be bolder?"

VI

Pearl rammed his shoulder against the wooden barrier
And knocked open a door just wide for Golems and Harps.
"I believe your push has worked, for I have been sent sailing.
Never mind the future of me; I shall fly here, stew and carp."
So came a fading rodent voice.
"Let's meet upon the stage and discuss our coloratura strategy,"
Shouted the Mouse.
"She seems certainly near; I hear her sound, soft and lofty,"
Said the Mouse, bouncing on the stage.

12

"I cannot... oof... wait to see... oof... her dress, her dance her... oof.
When she sings 'Oh dearest name,' I am such a... oof... softy."

VII

Fred looked longingly about the stage for his soprano star
And only heard a teasing breeze wheeze through the rafters.
"I hear chains rattle, a clank; I hear cooling lights snap, a pop."
But nowhere do I see bassos or altos, hear cries or laughter."
So said the Mouse, disappointed.
"I fear we'll never find Jo... Oh Jo! Oh Jo!"
Continued the Mouse.
"Find me by this magnificent light here on the stage.
Look how it casts shadows over the house, row after row."

VIII

Pearl and Jarry joined Fred in the empty theater
And saw their shadows cast tall by the lone ghost light.
"We've found the Everlasting Light again, in this Here's palace.
Have you ever seen such an essence, something so bright?"
So said the mesmerized Golem.
"Churn, Fred, churn fervid visions within your brain,"
Said the Golem.
"Imagine this globe here as your lofty moon.
Fred! Imagine your perched Queen, minding her heavenly reign."

IX

Fred heard rumbles in three stomachs
And suggested they search for the possibility of seeds.
"If you sift careful enough through this mounting dust,
You can find things quite delicious, satisfying your needs."
So said the Mouse.
"Golems are light eaters, Fred, I must admit,"
Said Pearl.
"We tend to dine from a more earthly table, finer clays.
But this here door may reveal goodies; volunteers for the gambit?"

All three hesitantly stepped towards the door
And read a sign above its threshold – 'Thou Shall not Enter the Cage'.
"I am in agreement with not entering, in any light, a cage.
Once inside, I know from memory, you'll be left in fit and rage."
So advised the Mouse.
"I shall pick the lock with my sharpest whisker,"
Plotted the Hare.
"This one, alone, once opened riches hid at Ft. Knox.
Don't believe me, fine; you needn't snarl or snicker."

The Golem, Mouse and Hare returned to the theater
And basked in the glow the commanding ghost light.
"Ah, Pearl! What have you done, letting loose a fermata?
Too many of those and it's going to be a long night."
So quipped the Hare.
"There is much music in a Golem Concerto,"
Returned Pearl, one-eyed with a large brow curved above it.
"I might stretch the legs a bit, you know, loosen the bellows.
Then with a downbeat cue I, like the seafaring breeze, will blow."

The Mouse requested a mazurka for he was a particular mouse,
And the Golem prepared by stretching and fine-tuning.
"You have your chances of stamping plus clicking.
The Rabbi loves the Chopin, lively, quite unassuming."
So mused the Golem.
"We'll have an odd circle of three,"
Answered the Hare.
"Hopping comes natural but Fred… his stamping…
His paws tap so lightly how will we match his impeccable tempi?"

The Golem played a holiday Tchaikovsky tune,
And Fred and Jarry and Pearl danced a mazurka.
"How did you learn this dance, such fine steps?
You've got a Cottontail's pep, like those from Alberta."
So asked the Hare of Fred.
"All must learn to jig in order to live,"
Answered Fred.
"The world has so many spiky things and gnashing teeth,
A Mouse is often slight, with only one life to give."

IV

The odd trio stomped and clicked under their special moon
And Pearl's clay bellows tooted a tune once inscribed to a Duchess Maria.
"Fred! In all honesty, there is no opera here or anywhere near.
The singers have gone silent, from Baton Rouge to Topeka."
So spoke the Hare.
"This Here is a Here for devoted, fanatical spirits,"
Noted the Golem.
"This Here is the Here for Butterflies and Night Queens.
Fred, set your highbrow beneath your eyebrow; you'll hear it."

XV

The Golem spun Fred on the ghost light by his trapezoidal tail,
And Pearl's toots crescendo skyward, ever so sharp.
"How do you muster so much wind, enough for every blade in Holland?
How do you stay in tune, snicker and pluck, like Cana's harp?"
So queried the Hare.
"My every burst is a burst for the joy of Here, Sir Hare,"
Replied the Golem.
"Fred is twirling and humming the brightest notes of Joe Green.
You are hopping and clicking; there is no better There out There."

I

A walrus waddles into a barber
And asks the barber for a trim.
"How can I make such beautiful follicles
All the more better, all the more slim?"
So asked the Barber.
"I'm looking for a new look, just for folly,"
Said the Walrus,
"Perhaps a Dutch Master 'stache
Or even an homage to dreamy Señor Dali."

Book II
Scene 1
Farzeenish

I

The Golem and the Hare and the Mouse basked in the light
And shared the lives of their own ghosts.
"I've memories of the ranging Splotched Cat,
Its white fur scattered, with patches of skin in sun left to roast."
So began the Mouse.
"In my memory, I lived between two forest realms,"
Said Fred.
"Towards a deep ravine were spiky locusts.
Away stood nothing but pines, plus one rather slippery elm."

II

Fred recalled the shape of the subject of his tale
And the haunting of Faded Orchard Gully.
"When moonless nights encased the Locusts,
Farzeenish rose from gravel and rocks, blistered, unholy."
So whispered Fred.
"His white coat torn, he walked with swagger, feline verve,"
Said Fred.
"All the street mice called him Fakakta.
But those who feared him the most called him Merv."

III

The terrified Hare held tight to the Golem's head
And left the impression that Pearl wore a new pompadour.
"Shorter names are best applied in times of peril.
Called out warnings should blast with letters less than four,"
Explained Fred.
"As lifelong student and fervent thinker of rodent reason,"
Continued Fred,

"When faced with brutal Cat Ghost cantankerousness
Use precise words like Run, Run, and, ever so loudly, Run!"

IV

The Mouse looked directly at his new friends
And spoke with candor, razor-sharp words.
"To say scuttle may turn you into a Farzeenish meal.
His arrival turned Mouse parties into rampaging herds."
So spake Fred.
"Farzeenish's flesh flaunted popping veins, jagged scars,"
Spake Fred even more.
"His slashed right blue eye squinted to say I spy lunch.
Calls of Merv! Merv! Merv! Gave petrified mice time to speed away far."

V

Jarry quivered upon Pearl's round head
And the Golem's pompadour started to shed.
"Such warnings seem to fail with regard to lawnmowers!
Or any other swinging blade aiming for one's head."
So remarked the Rabbit.
"Lawnmowers are unnatural things that seek only to devour,"
Said Fred.
"There's nothing to be said to stop swirling blades
Even by shouting Lawn and Lawn and Lawn for over an hour."

VI

Fred said the mice he knew gathered by the Locusts
And lived under a neighboring greying platform of wood.
"All the wood had splintered, season by season.
There, by night, we gathered for seeds, just loving 'Mice in a Hood.'"
So described Fred.
"When Farzeenish emerged, paw after paw, from the Gully bank,"
Said Fred.
"His muscular body outlined from a distant flashing light,
Farzeenish ordered the mice, one by one, to walk the plank."

The Golem's bottom bellows hooted from the fright
And Jarry's enormous ears twisted in a fantastic roll.
"Into my jaws! Into my jaws! I can swallow you whole!
Every available rodent, mouse, rat and mole."
So Fred quoted the nightmarish fiend.
"March into the gully that leads to my gut,"
Quoted Fred of Farzeenish.
"Come one to the edge of these woods
And fulfill my insatiable, no, unquenchable glut."

VIII

Fred spoke of the mice lining up to face their fate
And how he made the most important decision of his life.
"Father was a field mouse; his world ranged from Plank to Locusts.
That's where he was born, studied burrowing, and wed his wife."
So said Fred.
"He was quite disappointed that I chose to be a street mouse,"
Continued Fred, wiping a tear.
"But it was then and there that I chose to leave the Locusts,
Say farewell to faded planks and to my father's house."

IX

The Hare stepped forward lending a comforting paw
And he expressed a Rabbit's empathy and care.
"I doubt any stated difference between jaws and swirling blades.
Such threats are burdens we fur fellows continuously bear."
So said Jarry.
"But how in a Quadrupedalist's Green Earth did you manage to escape?"
Asked Jarry.
"I have to smile and say it was with a tear and a plucked whisker,
Then the trees would be our way out of this scrape."

X

The Mouse walked to the edge of the stage, raising his arms,
And his shadow stretched from Row C to the last, labeled YY.
"When we heard old Dart singing our blessed Mouse's Prayer,
'We thank the Spirit's gift of barley, wheat, and rye.'"
So recalled Fred of the prayer.
"Dart spoke boldly, standing in pools of Farzeenish drool,"
Continued Fred's account.
"'Ye though I go forth into the gully of a meadow mouser,
I dissolve sans fear, sans affront, my heart beats the cruel.'"

XI

Fred grabbed Dart's paw, before his friend took the plunge,
And pulled the faithful one away from the doomed hoards.
"Dear Dart, I've a better plan that starts with a whisker.
Be not a Farzeenish snack; let's arm with Locust swords."
So recommended Fred.
"Let's pluck the trees for a mounted offensive campaign,"
Advised Fred.
"With mouse muscle and grit, we pull off many thorns,
But with the crack of lung-sore thunder, it started to rain."

XII

The Golem started to laugh, launching his melodic bellows,
And he held tight to his jiggling belly, rolled and shout:
"Of course it should rain, Of course it should pour, HAR!
Does it not always rain when monsters are about?"
So howled Pearl.
"I shall never aspire to be this Cat's nosh-up then tubular poop,"
Declared Dart.
"I may be on the primrose path to digestion,
But I will march in a defiant and stately troop."

The Mice each plucked a whisker to annoy their foe
And jabbed their wiry growths between the cat's teeth.
"The gulley echoed with a cacophony of twangs
While others gathered Locust thorns into a lethal wreath."
So reported Fred.
"Dart took to the top of a tree, armed with jagged saws,"
Said Fred smiling.
"He slid down over dew settled on the slippery elm's trunk
Plunging the Locust swords squarely into Farzeenish's paws."

XIV

The Golem and the Rabbit roared and rolled over the stage
And dust blew up all over the storyteller.
"Farzeenish yelped and bounced and cried,
Disappearing deep into the gulley's dark, hellish cellar."
So said Fred.
"All the mice cheered and danced and pooped just the same,"
Smiled the Mouse.
"But I understood Farzeenish would almost certainly return.
So, I set out to be a street mouse and all the safety I could claim."

XV

The Mouse again stepped the stage's apron to raise his paws,
And dust roosted over his shoulders like a royal mantle.
"In the shadows of ghost light's reach a mouse can be king.
Gather all things cinematic that he can invent then handle."
So reflected the Mouse.
"Fred! You shared some coarse qualities a chilling tale requires,"
Said the Hare.
"Gnashing teeth and scaring cats and gapping gullies petrify!
But let me creep you all with pictures of old Satch McGuire."

Book II
Scene 2
Satch McGuire

I

The Hare stood on the edge of the stage with Fred
And shadows of his paws stretched towards the balcony's last seat.
"Listen carefully! Hear the essence every aria ever sung on this stage,
Every note, every expression, from Dvořák dances to the Scheherazade
suite."
So ruminated the Rabbit.
"Those tunes are not from the operas, not even by a stretch,"
Chimed in the Golem.
"Ha! You've made a mistake by far more than a hair.
You Kindly kinigl, You Sweet Little hozele! You fur-ball mensch!"

II

The Rabbit smiling, placed a paw upon Pearl's slumped shoulder
And he stared directly into the Golem's sunken face.
"As I said, Old Satch McGuire had a fence made of spiked wire,
And it stretched about an expansive, trapezoidal space."
So said Jarry.
"Many brown and grey rabbits were caught in Satch's fence,"
Said Jarry into the Golem's vacant sockets.
"Some were sent scurrying into the desert beyond.
Many dangled, crying for their lives, in wires sharp and dense."

III

Jarry cleared his throat of fur, phlegm, gnawed endive
And spoke of his home, brothers, and sisters.
"Old Satch sharpened his mower's blades daily…
Diamonded steel shredded steel in the shadow of a desert minster."
So recalled Jarry.
"From our nest, we could hear the squeal of his whetstone,"
Reflected Jarry.

"Grind! We huddle closer! Grind! We huddle tight! Grind! Grind!
In fear that the blade would be for us, each dawn we lay prone."

IV

Jarry tugged his ears straight, pulling out a thought,
And plucked away two vagrant lobe hairs.
"Satch screamed over his fence at each and every rabbit,
'Get on back to y'all's fields of origin, you dang, darn Hares!'"
So explained the Rabbit.
"But we carried whispers saying there were leafy harvests ahead."
So noted Jarry.
"Whispers of leafy harvests and safe fields from spinning blades,"
Continued the Rabbit.
"Gathered by a river running by the minster that was hardly a cathedral,
We gulped water, plotted a stampede, relished one last cool shade."

V

The Golem scratched his cavernous armpits
And, swatting away crumbles of clay, considered Jarry's cause.
"Out there, when there by the hardly cathedral, how to arm?"
"Oh Pearl, don't you know? We carried no arms, only rabbit paws."
So corrected Jarry.
"With no Locust thorns or mouse whiskers to call upon,"
Noted the Hare,
"We were left to the sweet sinew of our swift paws.
We gathered to charge for fertile grazing, with grit, with brawn."

VI

Jarry released his ears, followed with a twitch of his nose,
And Pearl and Fred twitched theirs, as well, with due respect.
"Before the dawn of rabbit stampede, we restlessly slept.
Nightmares were our only visions; we knew not what to expect."
So stage whispered Jarry.
"Then just as dawn broke, Satch's mower took us all by surprise,"
Said the Hare.

"Our nest shook, crabbed grass, shattered daisies flew overhead.
Alarmed my poor mother; her beautiful head did rise."

VII

Pearl rubbed his nose with golem dexterity,
And it popped away, tumbling then bouncing about the stage.
"It would be just my luck that the Here's air sits too dry for my clay.
But, I have not the inclination to chase after my nose, at my age,"
Groused the Golem.
"Leave your nose for another day; I am sure it will turn up,"
Admonished the Hare.
"I've blades to warn you about because they maliciously slice about.
Brother Jacque caught a blade slashing his foot.
Amidst Derecho winds, it was a damned Rabbit rout."

VIII

Jarry hopped lightly to a darkened wing
And choked words up into the palace loft.
"Poor Jacque, grabbed by Satch, tossed in a rusted tank,
Into a browning liquid. Jacque rolled; he coughed."
So said Jarry.
"Had I still a nose it would run along with my tears, as expected,"
Remarked Pearl.
"We'll find a nosebag to carry your running nose, dear Pearl.
Just imagine poor Jacque drowning in the muck of a septic."

IX

The Golem touched where once rested a ruddy schnozzle
And noticed a trickle of snot stretching from wing to wing.
"How does a nose move from a Here to another Here?
Better yet, how does a detached nose find such pitch to sing?"
Queried the Golem.
"Every stage has its mad spirits and howling beasts,"
 Interrupted the Rabbit.

"But far, far more vicious than the insatiable Farzeenish,
Satch McGuire plotted a winter's worth of grotesque feasts."

X

The Golem's nose scuttled past the light, humming Shostakovich,
And chuckled that his proboscis sprinted so spiritedly.
"Just before noon, the rabbits gathered for the much-needed cross.
It was an international gathering, born for those viewing safety
inquisitively."
So reported Jarry.
"With wildness, the Rabbits sped towards the greater terrestrial,"
Said Jarry.
"Some hopped, some galloped like the grand Jacks they were,
But when we launched upon Satch's barbed spears, we soon hung aerial."

XI

The Hare stepped into the Ghost Light's waving haze
And stood as the lone being visible in a light forest.
"Brothers and Sisters hung in wire like ragged November leaves,
Crying for aid and home like that old Hebrew Nabucco chorus."
So uttered the Hare.
"Satch McGuire snatched them all, tossing them in the tank with Jacque,"
Continued the Rabbit, furiously.
"There they huddled, shivering, by a spitting, hideous spout,
Until, grabbing their bunny feet, Satch proceeded to slice, to chop."

XII

The Golem's nose quivered in a corner of the stage
And filth puffed up all around as it spouted Golem sniffles.
"O World, to have to say goodbye to brothers and sisters.
It was then we saw an escape, one we had to take like missiles."
So said Jarry.
"The old spout ended its drizzle; it appeared completely dry,"
Continued the Hare.

"It was then and there we chose to make our way through its mouth,
One Rabbit after yet another, pumping paws at Satch to defy."

XIII

Jarry shrank from the ghost light's reach
And swatted dust bunnies from his grey tail.
"I hear the world about you mourning and wailing.
Your tale has made the earthworms in my shoulder cry,"
Said Pearl.
"My fleas, buried within my own fur, are shedding flea tears,"
Said Jarry with a small smile.
"The parasites and germs within the fleas are wailing.
As are their brothers, their sisters, their peers."

XIV

Fred emerged from Pearl's fallen nose nostril
And, quivering, he confessed his stage fright.
"Fellas! Some come as windbags, others merely fleabags!
Others are dirt bags pushing on me day and night."
So misquoted Fred.
"But this was a tale, by Jarry, that simply horrified,"
Stammered Fred.
"I'm sorry that, like some noses I know, I caused your flesh to crawl.
But the matter of swimming though the pipes! Us against the tide."

XV

Fred spotted a moth dancing about the ghost light
And sobbing along with all the fleas and germs.
"I've never ever actually seen a moth bawl
But I've seen many in webs twist and squirm."
So acknowledged Fred.
"I am now charged to say I have too many such tales,"
Noted the Golem.
"Granted, I seem to have a nose created to find trouble.
I am too inconsequential to answer all that trouble entails."

I

Pearl lifted the Mouse from his fugitive nose
And, with a finger, twirled snot off the rodent's coat.
"From this Here forward, I show you, my friend,
I shall protect you from Farzeenish; I give you my bon mot!"
So proclaimed the Golem.
"So too, Monsieur Jarry! I pledge to protect you from Satch McGuire."
So announced Pearl.
"As long as I maintain my clay, I will pledge in this palace;
No Rabbit will ever lose a hair or hang on Satch's barbed wire."

II

Fred and Jarry drew in stale stage air
And held their breaths, lest the Golem shock with different news.
"You must understand, Pearl, Satch grabbed my brother's feet,
To hang them on the key chain that opened a tank of refuse."
So said Jarry.
"With every breath I take of this lovely air,"
Said Pearl,
"I am made to defend all who wake daily defenseless.
I will be a quadruped's guard with golem care."

III

The Golem sensed the palace's specters, ghouls, elated fae,
And tucked his nose in his only available pocket – his ear.
"You have both added to my collection of ghosts, my haunting.
I know traps and pipes have made you as angry as you appear."
So mourned the Golem.
"Horrors led you to the life of a highway bunny, at the very least,"
Continued the Golem.

27

"But you, Jarry, are an incompetent crook.
I also know you have constantly failed to fleece."

IV

Jarry hung his face in slight shame, with rabbit guilt,
And swore to end his life as a hapless thief.
"Fellas of Fur! Promise never to pick the fight,
Then I will swear to protect you from further grief."
So vowed Pearl.
"Never natter or conspire with the yacking Night Hags,"
Advised the Golem.
"Keep key fingers close to your paw palms!
Don't chatter with the city's top gasbags!"

V

Fred rubbed his chin with a concerned paw
And considered how to correct a well-intentioned Golem.
"It seems to me that your heart glows with great intentions,
But mice and rabbits lack fingers; they even lack palms."
So corrected the Mouse.
"But since you mentioned something constantly yacking,"
Asked the Mouse.
"What in the concrete creation of the world
Might be a Night Hag? My knowledge is a little lacking."

VI

The Golem cracked the knuckles he brought along for this trip,
And tiny bits of reddish rock fell to the floor in crumbles.
"There are things out past this lovely palace that await us.
Those known as the Evil Eyes, creatures bringing all our troubles."
So warned the Golem.
"Point your ears only in my direction; never let your mind stroll,"
Presaged Pearl.
"I will say where an Evil Eye is cast; be quite prepared.
You came to this Here with skin, it will be your skin that shall crawl."

VII

Pearl let out a horrendous belly laugh
And he spoke of vile creatures, filled with operatic wrath.
"There are many forms for the Eye to take,
But once the Eye has been cast upon you, it's a damning path."
So said Pearl, his belly jiggling.
"Envy remains a friend to beyz agoyg, his greatest ally,"
Continued the Golem.
"We'll need special means to ward off such a nemesis –
To say kayn ayn hore or kaynahor, may there be no Evil Eye."

VIII

Fred walked as closer to the Golem as any mouse
And worked his way up clay legs and torso.
"Will we meet Envy once we leave this palace?
Will it be present outside those doors less or more so?"
Asked Fred, looking straight into the Golem's sockets.
"Envy sifts amongst the ghosts in this Here opera palace,"
Answered Pearl.
"In this Here's silence, Envy drifts forever as splintered spirits,
Saturday night phantoms, the remaining haze of old malice."

IX

Pearl crossed the stage to admire narrow wings,
And Fred rode along upon the Golem's slumping shoulder.
"Fred! Jarry! Prepare your right thumb for your left hand.
Then, place your left thumb in your right, tight then tighter."
So directed Pearl.
"Then say, 'as sons of Joseph, no Evil Eye shall send me shame,'"
Continued the Golem.
"Beware, for example, the likes of one Leo the Inhaler.
A river-bound fiend who for sucking up all joy earned his fame."

X

Pearl began to sniffle as he spoke of this creature, Leo,
And dust began to irritate the Golem's nose, still resting in his ear.
"Scratch my nose, if you please, Fred, for it itches.
Thank you, kind Mouse; please check to make sure my nostrils are clear."
So requested Pearl.
"I shall oblige, grand Golem, though your cavernous passages appear wet,"
Returned the Mouse.
"But I fear that I am hardly a son of a man you called Joseph.
My forefathers' names were Ed; each married foremothers named Yvette."

XI

Pearl raised his head to the rafters
And let go a moan of satisfaction as Fred scratched.
"I met Leo somewhere very near this very palace.
He looked me over, and his plotting quickly hatched."
So spoke the Golem.
"Each day I would look to guard those that I love with loves,"
Said Pearl.
"I would say, 'How happy you look! How beautiful you be!'
Yet Leo came, crushing each notion, each excitement, with vile verbal shoves."

XII

Jarry leaned against the ghost light pole
And flicked sawdust and grime from his nails.
"When we crawled through pipes on our way to freedom,
We met, in stench, floating, croaked toads, some as large as whales."
So chimed in the Rabbit.
"If I passed such horrors, emerge to find a privy as our gaoler,"
Boasted Jarry,
"Then, I can certainly hold my head and ears in defiance.
Then, I can certainly confront the bad behavior of Leo the Inhaler."

30

XIII

Pearl stomped, breathed heavily, snorted in vexation,
And determined snot blew from his nostrils at Fred.
"I speak with affection, with unabashed concern;
To be happy, Leo will turn on you, wishing you dead."
So thundered the Golem.
"Leo delights in your gloom; everything comes as a pall,"
Warned Pearl.
"There is a way to elude, to dodge his Evil Eye.
For Leo the Inhaler, no day should ever be droll."

XIV

Pearl spoke directly to his sleepy friends
And swamped each in his colossal palms.
"Pop in two scoops of bee's honey before you sleep.
Then, as your lids grow heavy, recite the exact Psalm."
So lectured Pearl.
"Before we leave this opera palace we must oppose the Evil Eye,"
Advised the Golem.
"With all you can muster, in tongue, nasal, and palate,
Summon harmonious spittle that to the left, right, and forward you'll let
fly."

XV

The Golem, the Mouse, the Rabbit spat to the right, then to the left,
And an air puff planted Pearl's thick gob upon the head of the Hare.
"Those in the back must always go with a pretend flow.
Now finish with a tremendous fountain, with all you have spare."
So instructed the Golem.
"In a special sea, we shall find a special fish… don't smirk… it's true,"
Advised Pearl.
"We'll search for the magnificent swimmer, Herr Lox.
Now let's leave this palace, cautiously, by shouting Ptoo! Ptoo! Ptoo!"

The walrus mused of illicit romances over a fish dinner
And flaked away pieces of salmon with his mighty walrus flipper.
"My ears collect, by chance, the whine of misguided suitors.
I hear, minute by minute, each moan, every wasted whimper."
So spoke the Walrus, between chews.
"But I've a whine, too, that may fade with the diary of Muse Clio,"
Said the Walrus.
"The beaches flamed, the fish grow slight, the deep end deeper.
These days forward, I need be ferocious, like a Greenland shark or Leo."

Book III
Scene 1
Shmuts

I

The Mouse, the Golem, and the Hare said farewell to the Ghost Light,
And Fred was the first to force his way out of the opera palace.
"I am sure… OOF… that this was… OOF… the same door… OOF… we entered.
I've squeezed… OOF… through so many walls… OW… my paws are callused."
So uttered the Mouse.
"From here, I can see the night's clouds, the sky's been draped nimbus,"
Said Fred.
"I can feel it! I can truly feel that it looks to be a fine day.
Your turn to come to the streets; best to exit first by your butts."

II

Pearl and Jarry exited the opera palace as instructed,
And the Golem bopped the Rabbit with his clay behind.
"Please excuse awkwardness of my curved earth.
Where have you gone, Jarry? Are you crushed by my girth and rind?"
So apologized the Golem.
"Oh, I am merely flattened upon your rind, it's magnificent girth,"
Said Jarry.
"My face is squished on you; we're riding cheek to cheek.
This is the worst arrival I've had since the day of my birth."

III

Pearl lost his footing, his backside heading toward the alley,
And he suddenly felt a jab by the crushed parking sign.
"Exiting by navigating Golem and Hare butts seemed unwise.
I have been called the Gormless Golem, words to which I resign."
So proclaimed the Golem.
"I rode a boat across to London for an all-golem seminar,"

Continued Pearl.
"There's where a Stamford Hill golem called me a Numpty.
These words I do not understand, but seemed on par."

IV

Jarry peeled himself off the Pearl-rutted backside
And patted his friend on his shoulder, headed in a slump.
"I am just a Rabbit from a field left in Montreal,
A cosmopolitan, fur-lined beast, stern, stately grump."
So chimed the Rabbit.
"But I know when a grand soul lives within a Golem,"
Said Jarry.
"As sure as a fresh cabbage shines greater than a sparkling diamond.
You look too far inward, you peer between your back blades. How
solemn."

V

Pearl stared at the alley with discerning sockets
And sniffled out of his nose, still resting his ear.
"It must be the seminars I've attended at Golem conventions,
'Beastly Epistles: The Modernist Monster', oh, too much to bear."
So mused the Golem.
"The saddest session was saved for the last,"
Recalled Pearl.
"It was called, to my horror, 'Golem Girls: Fact or Still Fiction.'
This one I left early, not slowly but ever so fast."

VI

Jarry cleared his throat, flicked a paw on the Golem's head,
And reminded his friends of their search to thwart the Evil Eye.
"You say we need to find the revered Herr Lox.
In what waters should we find such a rye and scaly guy?"
So questioned the Hare.
"On the river of your birth, Pearl, the muddy Scioto, rests our panacea,"
Professed Jarry.

34

"On its banks, there docked, is what was once called a carrack,
Which we should swipe, unfurl, and set sail – the aged Santa Maria.

VII

The Golem, the Mouse, and the Hare ran for the Scioto-moored ship
And ran under a slice of moon, barely hung over a streetlight prism.
"Let's beware the Broad Street breeze; its gust will blast you into distant flight.
You'll be searching for breakfast in Obetz, sadly uncharted Ohio tourism."
So advised the Hare.
"There's the dock. There's the boat. Let's board before another round of rain,"
Recommended Jarry.
"By finding Herr Lox, we can push away the years of the Evil Eye,
Rectify offences by sending this ligneous ship back to Spain."

VIII

Fred held on tightly to Pearl's pulpy leg,
And tumbleweed trash blew from the dock into the river.
"Don't be moving a muscle or a whisker, you be invading cruds,
Or my fellows will be chowing down on you all, be lung and liver."
So shouted a red-eyed rat.
"You must be Leo, the Inhaler, by noise emanating from your snout,"
Said Jarry.
"I neither be a Leo nor be such an inhaler, nor be a noisemaker.
I be Shmuts, a wharf rat, guarding dock, ship, keeping you be cruds out."

IX

Fred once again, shamefully, publicly pooped from fright
And, ashamedly, poked the turd away with a hind paw.
"We are seeking to thwart the Evil Eye and perhaps find Soprano Jo.
We seek Herr Lox. Oh lord, you are the ugliest wharf rat I ever saw."
So confessed the Rabbit.
"I be HA! HA! HAWING! 'cept I can tell you, there's no Herr Lox here, Hare,"

Interrupted Shmuts,
"For our wharf labor all get carp for a diem,
Straight from the bottom of this Scioto there!"

X

The Golem spied crowds of Shmuts's cousins encroach,
And Fred wished to hear his Jo sing again, one so beloved.
"I need warn you, I've hardly the lung or liver for a decent rat's meal.
Worse, my rock fellow here would only be morsels of river mud."
So said a quivering mouse.
"Ah, a rabbit stew, however, would be a compliment to nightly carp,"
Said Shmuts.
"Be thinking that your pebbled friend looks to be a rat's plate,
A sprinkle of mouse innards on Hare! Voilà! A meal none too tart."

XI

Shmuts led the rats all the more closer to the trio,
And spittle flew out from his protruding chopper.
"I be in desire for a scrumptious, tender nose to start!
To be gnawing at the rabbit nostrils, Yum! Gravy à la Macabre."
So drooled, Shmuts.
"Tell your salivating cousins they would wish for a Rabbitical scholar to live,"
Chimed in Jarry.
"Scholar my jagged paws; I shall nibble you down to a Hare cob.
I care for nothing as I even have a rat's ass to give."

XIII

The Golem pulled his nose from his ear, firing up a champagne cork pop,
And, with a leg kick wind-up, bounced the ruddy rock off the rat's head.
"Devour this, you misshapen river sod, you revolting bunch of beastliness.
I've a nose for the fight business, and will be your daily, no, your nightly dread."
So shouted the Golem.
"BEGAD! BEGAD! BEGAD! My noddle's got newly, rising lump,"

Screamed Shmuts.
"HA! HA! HAWING! Shmuts pooped! Allow my sharpest mouse whisker be plucked.
Tip it off with a fresh Shmuts turd, with which I'll jab, then return it to your rump."

XIV

Pearl's nose ricocheted off Shmuts, taking out seven other rats,
And flew right back into the Golem's Koufax–like palm.
"Here's a swift kick for the rest of you and the other rest of you.
Knocking your rat selves is soothing, a street Hare's balm."
So flailed the Hare.
"Run you creepy-crawlies, evil alley vampires, wretched parasites!"
Bellowed Jarry.
"Skip to the slivered moon, to the planets beyond. Here's a night to rue.
Sooth your pains on Mercury; just flash, flash out our sight."

XV

Shmuts howled and hollered, soared into the night,
And vanished, a mouse whisker wiggling from a most obscene spot.
"That's a whisker bender if I've ever heard one.
I would slap my knees if I had a few; Shmuts can all go and rot."
So boasted the Mouse.
"The coast is now clear to board the floating Santa Maria,"
Spoke out Pearl.
"Aboard, we'll sail the Scioto to an Ohio, on to the Mississippi & the great Gulf,
Around the Florida horn to the Atlantic; there goes us by nautical schema."

Book III
Scene 2
A Santa Maria Cruise

I

Pearl examined the Santa Maria deck sternly,
And brownish water lapped delicately at its bow.
"HA! Old Shmuts was bopped on the bow, poked in the stern.
Jarry, my Rabbitical hero, you hulled up, winning the rats row."
So proclaimed the Mouse.
"One swift kick and those nasty fellows just keeled over,"
Boasted Fred.
"Fred, gnaw away the mooring so we can find a way to set sail.
A righteous wind is needed to make this ship a river rover."

II

Fred set to work chewing away at plastic ties,
And teeth clattered more than twice upon the iron cleat.
"Oh! That is a feeling that really smarts. I believe I hear chickens.
But, how many knots shall we travel by, in this one ship fleet?"
Asked the Mouse.
"Only two, one for each shoe, as any more… too difficult to unfurl,"
Replied the Golem.
"Now, look above as we leave this city port, see the stars revealed.
Sailor's delight! Let's give the Santa Maria one grand whirl."

III

Pearl pulled together his clay bellows tightly
And ripped a wind that bowed sails, all three masts.
"How the street signs all bend in deference to your gale.
Pearl, that was quite the gastroenterological blast."
So complimented the Hare.
"Despite voices to the contrary, there is a place for Golem methane,"
Replied Pearl.

"Take watch, up in the castle, navigators Fred and Jarry.
I'll turn a rudder from this stern pulpit, once we open the main."

IV

The Golem, the Rabbit, the Mouse felt the ship jerk towards Spain
And quickly come to a halt as brownish water splashed up the port.
"What holds us back, other than fear of what comes next?
Someone has grabbed us from the depths; it's stopped us short."
So said the Golem.
"From this tall nest, it behooves me to be no less than franker,"
Said the Jarry, leaning seven inches towards the mast.
"Oh Oof! I've thumped my head on the Santa Maria's elevated lore.
Now I hear chickens and the muddy drag of our anchor."

V

The Santa Maria drifted with the current, not mention Pearl's wind,
And the anchor dredged up old Ohio buried in the river's muddy floor.
"Again, I hear clucking, vibrant cackling, plus a newborn baby's cry!
Lord in Heaven with a box score! Our anchor has opened the spiritual
world door."
So exclaimed the Hare, from the Castle.
"How the sky has bloomed with hens, floating about as Scioto Sirens!"
Reported Jarry.
"Hens of all sorts, flocking with a wretched man who says he's Jeremiah
Butes!
A chicken too many, in my mind, means the macabre in these environs."

VI

The Golem, along with the Mouse, scratched trembling knees,
And Jeremiah Butes' ghost spoke to the troika on the scud.
"These beautiful birds are the lost souls, Farmer Mead's Hens,
Whom, at Easter 1913, flew the coup lest they drown in a great flood."
So spoke Butes' ghost.
"Behold the spirit of policeman and mourning son, Harry Keys,"
Continued Jeremiah.

"He stumbled, with slouched shoulder, carrying his mother over waters,
Only to have river's slapping hands swipe his poor mother to sea."

VII

Jeremiah rose above the moored Santa Maria
And rained ectoplasm all about the ship's deck.
"I've all the more phantoms to show you, Golem, Mouse, Hare.
I need show you all who perished in the Meek Street wreck."
So argued the spirit.
"Have such poor souls inherited any of the Earth, these Ghosts of Meek Street?"
Asked Fred, shyly.
"One crushed into a riverbed inherits only mud in their still eyes.
Say, Mouse… slight Mouse… Allow me to be kind, spiritually discreet."

VIII

Jeremiah continued his lecture and levitation over the Santa Maria
And cast a pall over the shivering Mouse, staring straight into Fred's eye.
"You are stealing away, nay, returning history a la this false ship.
You must heed the clucks of our river goddess, Lorelei."
So proclaimed the Meek Street Ghost.
"She has the wisdom, nay the way, to find your gilled hero, Herr Lox,"
Screeched Jeremiah.
"More precise than a plodding, rafters of turkeys
Do admire this, this feathered shade, as she talks."

IX

A fierce-looking hen took Jeremiah's place above the thieving boodle
And eyed each mariner before she cleared her throat to say,
"Seek the Geese of Pee Pee Creek, who swim blissfully by the Muskie!
There, you will find the fish you seek, highlighted by a heavenly ray."
So advised the transparent Hen
"When you approach Herr Lox, be watchful the words you chat,"
Warned Lorelei.

"Never utter smoke, tomato, onion, capers, nor suggest eggs.
Restrain from commenting on the décor of his underwater flat."

X

The spectral fowl flapped her wings for statelier height
And, just as quickly she appeared, Lorelei faded into the night.
"Forever remember! Seek the Geese of Pee Pee Creek!
Bring kindness only to Herr Lox! Please him to the gills and be polite!"
So echoed the Hen throughout the Scioto.
"Forever remember! Chickens don't have fingers! Chickens don't have fingers!"
Said the ethereal Lorelei.
"Follow this dream until it becomes a fabulous wishbone,
Then gently snap into the right course, for now I can no longer linger."

XI

Mead's famed forlorn fowl vanished, leaving a wisp of her plume,
And the three sailors mused over Lorelei's 'fabulous wishbone'.
"This Here appears all the more odder than the opera palace.
Certainly, a wishbone holds as lofty goal, but her tone! Her tone!"
So mused the Golem.
"The Senorita Maria seems to be moving on her own might,"
Noticed an alarmed Jarry.
"We're sliding down... we've crushed a floating stage... stream!
Oh, our speed recalls Pee Pee Creek! Hold on tight!"

XII

Fred bumped his head into the boat's bow, inspiring a mountainous lump,
And was suddenly overcome by craving for a delightful pasta crunch.
"Oh, my middle whisker for Franchi seeds over uncooked rigatoni!
Oh, craving gods, why now should I hanker for such a midnight lunch?"
So said the insatiable Mouse.
"Oh, to then dine over such a supper with dear Soprano Jo,"
Fantasized Fred, revisiting his romantic side.

"A whole night as she whispers to me, 'Caro Nome, sweet Fred! Caro Nome!'
My heart swells. Flutes carol all about me! Allegro moderato!"

XIII

Fred rubbed his wounded head, watching the river waters divide,
And imagined flutes sounded off more like chickens clucking up high.
"The knots we achieve can by credited to gritty, say ghostly fowl.
I can see we are, once again, visited by the spirited Lorelei."
So observed the Hare.
"The hens have come to guide Maria's planks over to the right creek,"
Said Jarry.
"What odd formations these hens have come to make.
Why, they seem to fly with as a letter C – curved, yet so sleek."

XIV

Lorelei led a flock of ghost chickens across the river's sky
And pulled along the Santa Maria, in search of Herr Lox.
"For your questing pleasure, we shall highlight the sights!
There's the Ville of Massive Pumpkins, greater than gold in Fort Knox."
So clucked the ghost Hen.
"On shore, hear the Sycamores grumble, 'these dang carp tickle my root,'"
Narrated Lorelei.
"The Locust whisper back, 'their annoyance you can take to the bank!'
But the itch I feel, I fear, is a world of dry; I'll wind up a pile of soot."

XV

Lorelei and her company flew on, despite a quick change in the air,
And house lights flickered at airborne, clucking chickens, louder as any passing rig.
"Through April, June, and July, waters reached far above my knotted trunk.
Who's to blame for such deep waters? Why, I'll smack them with my first sprig!"

42

So Lorelei quoted a distraught Buckeye.
"The waving trees seem to be ready to dispute; it's a regular forest brawl,"
Reported Pearl.
"This Scioto bends after bends, changes sky color without notice.
The Hen Aeronautical Coterie have flown straight into a November Scioto squall."

Scene 3
The Geese at Pee Pee Creek

I

Jarry darted down from the Castle in three bounds,
And, within an available barrel, Pearl with Fred hid.
"This Scioto Squall comes with the complete package!
Ice packs a mighty punch... a Derecho perhaps! Heaven forbid!"
So called out flustered Hen.
"Call me Fred!! Mates! Thar's a great white sandbar on the Bow! Stern!!
No, Port!"
Shouted an alarmed Mouse from the barrel.
"Oh, this barrel wants to roll with the wind... Left! No, right! ... No, left...
oof!
More like a roller coaster; my stomach's dropped... not ... good... fort!"

II

The Derecho winds made the barrel to more rattle than roll,
And Pearl turned green enough for one to think he grew his own moss.
"Lend me your hat, Fred. I've need to leave my old lunch in its knits!
Oh, my. Here it comes, good and thick with a special clay gloss."
So puked the Golem.
"Oh, Pearl! That's not my hat but my damaged mouse head,"
Said an appalled Fred.
"Oh, to be under floorboards, munching on moldy chocolate.
My voracious desire for pasta is now officially dead."

III

Pearl profusely apologized to his friend for his impolite purge
And held the Mouse, lest he be tossed into the river.
"I've got you, Fred, by your tail; this wind shall clear my repulsive mess.
The indecency of puking on my little pal leaves me to shiver."
So called out the Golem.
"Don't feel the need to apologize, though my top is now slightly mauve,"

Said Fred.
"The swelling upon my head seems to be easing; oh, it's soothing.
Why, Pearl, for want of a better word, we'll call yours a heave salve."

IV

Jarry cringed at the jabber between Mouse and Golem,
And watched a greenish boat, loaded with honey, float by.
"Uh-Hey! Mr. Owl! How far to the Pee Pee? Oh! Greetings to your Miss Cat!
You serenade much like a chummy Daltrey, Hoo! Hoo! Quite sly!"
So called out a befuddled Bunny.
"Strange lovers traverse these waters after midnight,"
Shouted Lorelei to her stunned passengers.
"We meet new ones with each fowl haunting.
How lovely they all appear even without any moonlight."

V

Ohio pushed out the maelstrom, bringing forth obscured stars,
And the Derecho gave way to cold air, accompanied by a fabulous brass
section.
"Seek! Seek! Seek! Pee! Pee! Pee! Cats! Cats! Cats!
Sand! Sand! Six! Six! Six! Clock! Clock! Dive! Dive! Direction! Direction!"
So honked the floating brass ensemble.
"Seek! Seek! Seek! Pee! Pee! Pee! Fish! Fish! Fish!"
Said the Coro Geese of Pee Pee Creek.
"Engage! Engage! Squeeze! Squeeze Bowels! Bowels!
Dive! Dive! Bomb! Bomb!! Boat! Boat! Dish! Dish! Dish!"

VI

Pearl, Jarry, Fred, even Lorelei, all looked skyward
And heard in the solemn darkness the blasts, honking bogies.
"Whistles fill my ears, shrill warnings for what might be falling.
Duck! All feathered or furred, here comes torpedo poop trophies."
So shouted the Golem.
"Oh, the humanity! Heavy Skies! This is all she wrote!"
Warned Pearl.

"Seek! Seek! Seek! Pee! Pee! Pee! Cats! Cats! Cats
Dive! Dive! Dive! Bomb! Bomb! Bomb!! Boat! Boat! Boat!"

VII

Pearl, with renewed courage, peered over the portside
And spied his own rabbi in a rowboat, chanting the Shema.
"Sirens! That's what they must be! Duck! No, Geese!
First wind and ice, now geese and scheisse! Fates! What chutzpah!"
Proclaimed the oppressed Golem.
"I've defended against the grotesque, thumbed clay thumbs at fear,"
Reasoned Pearl.
"What can a man of clay fear? A soaking rain I suppose. Loneliness?
Ah! To be shat upon again and again, piled up all the way to the ear."

VIII

The Golem covered his ears which, incidentally, conveniently, covered his
nose,
And the world bombarded him and his friends with muck.
"Goose droppings are rattling on the deck like a Richard Starkey
backbeat!
Who ever thought Geese could play horn and percussion, soulful yet
punk?"
So admired the Hare.
"These missiles fall with great vigor, from my mouse perspective,"
Said Fred.
"One sore lump on my head is one sore lump too many;
A lump from geese projectiles hardly seems festive."

IX

A third boat passed the mariners, carrying a lady called Tallulah,
And dragged a young man named Jack, holding tightly on to its stern.
"Do all these river rowers seek Herr Lox, to thwart the Evil Eye?
It suggests there is a lot to worry over, much too much concern."
So mused the Golem from his place of safety.
"Here, we duck foulness cascading from the air,"

46

Thought Pearl.
"There, Tallulah rows by, statuesque, so frighteningly beautiful.
There goes along Jack, fully a nebbish, but with charisma to spare."

X

The Santa Maria, without helm, zigzagged the narrow river
And slammed to a stop on the great white sand bar.
"HO! HO! I knew your clumsiness would fulfill my destiny!
Ha! Ha! I have abandoned every great sinking ship so far."
So came a voice from under the ship's deck.
"Yet, I've never fled the dear Maria, a record I now sponge,"
Continued the rodent-like voice.
"It started with The Bounty, old Bligh, a burning at Pitcairn.
Yes, first Bligh then the Berg and the Titanic plunge."

XII

Snow, along with piercing winds, followed the malodorous storm,
And Lorelei began to fade into the November night.
"The great flood spared us all from the butcher's knife!
We recede content; you are clearly within Herr Lox's sight."
So said the vaporous Hen.
"Tell all children a Hen's wishbone sustains only a Hen's wishes,"
Said Lorelei, barely visible.
"To be a Hen for the fortunate sake of being a Hen;
It's our daily desire, rather than to become succulent dishes."

XIII

The Santa Maria came to a rest on the shining sand bar,
And the stranded trio watched the hens fade into the mist.
"Here's an island for paws; step forth, Golem, Scioto's Caliban.
Be careful for mischievous fae; it's Herr Lox we need enlist."
So mused the Hare.
"This soft sand feels much like it could be a Golem's home,"
Said Pearl.
"These clams I claim to know; these shingles shape like my feet.

With such comfort like these, I need no longer roam."
XIV

Jarry hopped from the ship's crushed bow
And found comfort in the bank's tall, brown grasses.
"My brother, Jacque, would have loved this cozy place.
Such long lawns… we could, fearlessly, watch for whatever passes."
So ruminated the Rabbit.
"Here! The remains of trillium… no, dead lobelia… no, butterfly weed!"
Shouted Jarry.
"So much to hide within, and cattail for daily spying.
Farmer's bales of which two or three, I promise to exceed."

XV

Fred made his departure from the marooned Maria
And he ran down the ship's splintered bow.
"There's that dang voice, following us, that's not a hen's.
It's a deeply harsh voice, not opera tunes beneath my brow."
So stated a concerned Mouse.
"Hop lightly, Hare! Stomp quietly, Golem, watch those wooden spikes, Mouse,"
Quote Fred of the voice.
"He says so much more of sinking ships, plus evenings hearing Puccini.
Well, random is random, which says old Shmuts roams Maria's house."

Sleep Cinematic Olio #3

The Walrus ran from home to the coldest coast in Norway
And there, he raised canine pups to the size of hairy worms.
"On this ice path, I'll love these fellows, lest winds blow them to the
Barents Sea.
Then I'll fish by the red-striped Slettnes Lighthouse's concrete berms."
So said the spiritual escapee.
"I shall scratch behind the ears of your Collie faces,"
Said the Walrus.
"Should we fail to finally breathe, we'll thieve air like Artic jaegers.
Then at night, we'll pack together for warmth inside cardboard
pillowcases."

BOOK 4
Scene I
The Legend of Emile

I

With cramped legs, Shmuts emerged from a wooden crate
And stood above the trio standing on the sand.
"I see you… Cramp! Have all your faith… CRAMP! In Herr Lox stopping the Eye!
You're a bag of gullible bumpkins, to believe a fish so grand."
So taunted the hampered rat.
"Through your haste… OW! I have finally… OW! Accomplished my quest!
CHARLIE HORSE!"
Shouted a strained Shmuts.
"Oh, my leg! Oh, my other leg! Oh, my back left leg! Oh, my other back leg!
What I thought was an ingenious hiding nest, I look at now with only remorse."

II

Pearl, Jarry, even a startled Fred roared with laughter,
And Shmuts rolled about the sand to loosen four strained rat calves.
"I have giggles and I have itches; I believe I've poison ivy in November.
Shmuts' dance is a joy, but these rashes need soothing salves."
So uttered the Golem.
"It was once said, rats fleeing a burning house suggests a truth to reveal,"
Spoke up Shmuts.
"Therefore, it is only a matter of rodent kindness
That I thus confess my legendary birth name – Emile!"

III

Along with the Golem, Hare, Mouse, all neighboring birds stood silent
And reflected on the moniker, Emile, before laughing aloud again.
"I know of a Zola or a de Becque but never a rat called Emile.
Your smugness leaves, from such hilarity, my stomach in pain."
So said the Hare, wiping away a tear.

"Over the years, the challenge to flee rotting house lost its luster,"
Continued Shmuts or, should it be said, Emile.
"So, I called all brother and sister rats to a conference.
I spoke for a decree to be change policy, without rodent filibuster."

IV

Shmuts stepped down from the decaying Santa Maria
And found a natural soapbox above the river's bank.
"All rat constituents decided, then, to only flee sinking ships,
To offer, from afar, bye-byes to captains, as their bodies sank."
So narrated the proud rat.
"Flee-missions began with the famed voyage of 1492,"
Began Emile.
"Some siblings gambled on the Nina, others on the Pinta.
I chose the latter, while it was lovely Maria that sank in the blue."

V

Emile cleared his throat, emptying sadness onto a dismayed crowd,
And he gave raucous testimony to a rat's ahistorical quest.
"Henceforth, I swore I would flee every great sinking ship.
This I pursued, heart plus soul, like a rat possessed."
So preached the rat.
"Edward Teach, My next great friend, dead from twenty fiendish sword strokes,"
Narrated Emile.
"My history may be sorely misconstrued due to all the years gone by
But, from the Revenge I flew, as it crashed into a sandbar near Ocracoke."

VI

Pearl's earthen eyebrows furrowed with solemn skepticism,
And he sought exact words to call Shmuts' bluff.
"You, you dirty rat, are in the Here, now, not in the Then, now.
Columbus! Teach! The same, rat? Your perspective seems a tad rough."
So argued the baffled Golem.
"Golem! My life, like my cousins, began at sea on a floating plastic heap,"

Replied Emile.
"Strange as it may seem, the years have given me awful names.
Emile, the Rancid! Emile, the Oceanic Fibber! Emile, the Seafaring Creep."

VII

Emile slipped a little on the bank, with back paws peddling for balance,
And he swallowed his minute humbleness, stroking his wired whiskers.
"There's much to behold on miles of drifting plastic bags and rings.
Such trash creates the tie that binds, much like apples, toast, and frayed knickers."
So reflected the legend.
"I flew when Captain Smith had his celebrated North Atlantic iceberg scrape,"
Related Emile.
"I said farewell to Astor, to Guggenheim, sailed away beside Molly Brown.
A tragic scene… 'The itty-bitty children losing lives'… quite the chilly escape."

VIII

Jarry now lifted his brows in mammal disbelief
And whispered his doubts into Pearl's ear and nose.
"There's something about this fellow's tale that fails to add up.
If he sallied forth from that ship, certainly his life and tail froze,"
Considered the discerning Rabbit.
"I was actually fortunate that my tale continued without strain,"
Interrupted Emile.
"If I had not been vacationing in Italia, hearing Puccini's new bohemians,
Then I would have been ready, that same night, to flee the Maine."

IX

Fred's eyes grew wide, relishing an inspired earworm of Giacomo,
And delightful voices filled his voracious brain.
"Oh Puccini! Puccini! Every house need say something of Puccini.
Only Puccini can make a winter scape seem warm, with such refrain."
So said a jumping Mouse.

"Puccini on the beach! Puccini in the bank! Puccini in Madagascar,"
Shouted Fred.
"It should be Puccini, Puccini! Puccini here plus everywhere!
Oh, how mighty that you were there, dear friend Edgar."

X

Emile snarled, looking to correct his rodent counterpart,
And he stepped directly over the elated Mouse.
"You mean to say Emile, restive, nutty runt.
Of course, I was there, as I am usually in an opera house."
So sputtered the raconteur.
"I may be by nature a rat, but even rats embrace high culture,"
Said Emile.
"My legend rests not with operas but with operatic sea tragedies.
I balloon, expanding as a minstrel of fabulous myth & vulgar."

XI

Emile took two steps backwards, then jumped from the bank
And, grabbing Fred, dragged a clawed paw across the Mouse's throat.
"Here you all stand, pinning your faith on a fish to correct your own ways!
Faith in my truth is all you need, my every tome, my every mote."
So said the insistent prevaricator.
"As a reminder, I had flown from every doomed ship save one,"
Snarled Emile.
"Black Swan… Mary Rose… the HMS this and that! Ah! Frozen
Endurance…
All but Saint Maria, I flew from thumbing a paw, all for joy,all for fun."

XII

Emile breathed with satisfaction, having finally flown the Santa Maria,
And drew his sharpest claw across Fred's neck.
"Farzeenish! Farzeenish has returned! Farzeenish is at my back.
I must break… Oof… free… from this rat's… Ow… grip… Heck!"
Hollered the frightened and choked Mouse.
"Say, Emile. You seem to be shedding bits of dust and grass,"

Shouted Jarry.
"Your very essence is flying off into the Pee Pee Creek breeze.
All that falls off you reveals that you are simply an ass!"

XIII

Emile took pride in the insult, pierced Fred's brown fur,
And let blood dribble down the Mouse's chin.
"Silence! You Quebecoise quiff! Do you see your mystical fish?
Look deep into the creek! Do your see Herr Lox's salmon skin?"
So snorted the maniacal Rat.
"As for you, Mouse! I knew Puccini better than most!"
Said Emile.
"I ate the words off his lined sheets, leaving only some humming.
I say, nothing tastes better, save globs of jam on rye toast."

XIV

Pearl's veins filled with Golem inclination,
And he stepped forward to flick Emile away.
"As a figure of earth and compassion, I need protect Fred.
Tale by tail your legend stirs pots, friction, utter dismay."
So said the Golem, smacking Emile air born.
"I rise like the rosy sun I see emerging to the east,"
Said a high-flying Emile.
"How does one rat flee so many ships? Trust me! I spiel nonsense into truth.
When a rat flees, he leaves you a sinking ship ride, at the very least."

XV

Emile's voice trailed off into silence as an Owl snared him with its talons
And swept the infamous rat away into gastrointestinal infamy.
"One can only wonder how Shmuts spent centuries as idiom star.
He's a myth! He's a bore! He's a legend! He's crank! The iconic Emile...
pure antinomy."
So pondered Jarry.

"It's best that we search for Herr Lox, leaving these worries for others to wrestle,"
Said Pearl.
 "Shmuts is off to a nest, singing how singular he might be,
For that must be true, now that he lays as an Owl's breakfast special."

Book 4
Scene 2
Herr Lox and Geese

I

Forty happy geese landed on the sandbar, surrounding the marooned troupe,
And profusely apologized for their late Pee Pee Creek arrival.
"Let me just say there is a tremendous fowl logjam on the border.
Attitudes toward migrating Canadian honkers seem quite tribal."
Said one outspoken goose.
"That's quite the mess you have brought to our marsh paradise,"
Continued the Spokes-Goose.
"Great fish loafers say, 'one is never alone when sunk on the ocean floor.
Eventually, all such bottom dwellers receive visitors more than once,
sometimes thrice.'"

II

The Goose hooted, honked, rolled mirthfully through his tragic absurdity,
And then queried the Golem as to what brought his entourage to the creek.
"We've come to call on Herr Lox to help us ward off the Evil Eye.
We've roamed opera palaces, swiped a little boat, yet all looks bleak,"
Bemoaned the Golem.
"Sadly, we must all admit that we've no sense of the humors of Herr Lox,"
Chimed in Jarry.
"Do we search saying, 'what's a fine fish like you doing in a creek like this?'
Or do we query the cold muskies carping about the rocks?"

III

Forty Geese called a Geese conference upon the bank,
And there was such chatter, Pearl's ear and nose began to ache.
"I fear these gentlemen took a run turn on the way to a deli.
If we had the means, we'd nip kippers and rye, good bread to break."
So spoke the Head Goose.

"In my time, the herring was far superior, sans canned, sans cream,"
Said an older bird amongst the flock.
"These days, one pops a tin and out comes a mesa of water and fish,
Not that I am ever invited to such events, not in my wildest dream."

IV

The elder geese pecked at the Spokes-Geese,
And an explosion of condemnation flowed through the Pee Pee reed.
"What do you know of delis or fish, you old goose?
These are the newer times, as true as my name is Pigweed!"
So shouted the assailing fowl.
"Are you, sir, the gooseherd amongst these raucous geese?"
Asked Pearl.
"The spirits of great chickens sent us to this spot in pursuit of Herr Lox.
Certainly, you have divine answers… that is, should your bickering cease."

V

A crackle from above signaled the collapse of Maria's sails,
And they snapped away the gooseneck from its mast.
"Such thunder on November morning won't do.
The Evil Eye creeps in every brook and creek, despotism my forecast."
So pleaded the Hare.
"I have seen the walls of such a trap, steely, cold, a prison,"
Added Fred.
"The food is similarly rotten, with spoiled Havarti the common dish.
Nor does one ever hear a harmonica blare or a Cash song; watch for the mizzen!"

VI

The crowd on Pee Pee beach scurried in wrong directions,
And rope, mast (with mizzen) crashed upon not fowl, rodent, rabbit, but on clay.
"I have caught the debris with my face, with no harm to my proboscis.
This is the day I celebrate a schnoz in the ear! This is the day!"
So boasted the Golem with splinters about his cheeks.

"Oh where were you when the mower came for Jacque's head,"
Asked Jarry.
"Say, from the corner of my eye I see orange flashes within those muddy waters.
Could that be Herr Lox rambling over tired stones on the riverbed?"

VII

An impressed Spokes-Goose waded a webbed foot in the river
And counted the ways Pearl would be written into the Book of Life.
"Do I hear an angelic harmonica playing ghostly tones?
Has Herr Lox come to award Pearl for his bravery through strife?"
So asked Fred.
"It appears there is something of a brighter color coming our way,"
Answered the Spokes-Goose.
"Yet salmon colors appear as red, on occasion pink.
What you see are bits of Golem flesh torn, floating as a river display."

VIII

Pearl's knees began to buckle from the broken mast mass,
And his facial features chipped, flacked, ached.
"A modest request for the morning, I'd like to take this mast off my mug.
This will call for a day at the Golem spa, a divine mudpack break."
So spoke up the Golem.
"I'll hold this splinter while you ease away from the pole,"
Advised Fred.
"If you have patience, I can take out this weight one sliver at a time.
When I have cleared enough chips, give this sailor's staff a little roll."

IX

Pearl's feet slipped on wet goose droppings, from previous night's deluge,
And the mast slid off into the water, smashing muskies on to the beach.
"Ah! My feet slide away on foul tubular meteorites.
In this Here, I am freed from Maria's crush, this cumbersome pastiche."
So exclaimed the Golem.

58

"Pardon the mess about your feet; old Pigweed had a gas attack midflight,"
Explained the Spokes-Goose.
"We were on our morning commute from Yoctangee to the Pee Pee,
When the poor fellow was once hit by his longstanding blight." HONK!

X

Pigweed pinched the Spokes-Goose's tail feathers,
And a high-flying Muskie landed, mouth open, swallowing up Fred.
"Ah! A musty Muskie has inhaled me whole.
Miles of travel and triumph, only to become a Fish's bread."
So cried a muffled Mouse.
"Oh, has there ever been such darkness in a mouse's world?"
Lamented Fred.
"I'm the Pee Pee Creek Jonah, its Geppetto, consumed by a whale.
Fare thee well beloved soprano Jo; Oh! How Fate has me furled."

XI

Pearl reached to rescue Fred but fell to the sand, laughing,
And a distraught Mouse staggered about with a Fish Crown.
"This night has given this monster blessings on blessings,
New friends, the cleaning of Shmuts, a boat ride beyond renown."
So chirped the Golem.
"This gilled masque does not conceal a Mouse at Carnival,"
Explained Fred.
"I suppose, on a more pleasant day, I could be the trickster Zanni.
But on this cold, wet morning, I am merely a Mouse, fully in the fish esophageal."

XII

Pearl examined sun reflecting off Fred's claustrophobic fish house
And rescued the distraught Mouse from his eternal darkness.
"Fred! On what *scale* would you rate your event?
I don't wish to *carp* on the matter, though I digress!"

So teased the Golem, joyful that he had saved yet another.
"Now that I am *fin*-ished, I will leave the matter, *swimmingly*,"
Giggled Pearl.
"Now, Mouse, why pout when snow covers the beach?
Ah! Fred! Please! Please, laugh with Jarry, the Geese, and me."

XIII

Jarry wretched at the Golem's misplaced puns
And briefly considered returning to his faux life of crime.
"I can steal away into the night when I hear such quips.
For a ruminating Hare, such quips cerebrally stick as intellectual grime."
So complained the Rabbit.
"Turn your attention to the river and its pieces of Golem,"
Suggested Jarry.
"What is to be expected when we now find there is no Lox?
What ways to cure the Eye, when there is no proper totem."

XIV

Fred looked at his paws, assured that he was himself again,
And he counted his nails, twice, then divided forty by four.
"My cuticles seem to outnumber the usual Mouse nail count.
Mice do well by multiplication, but division always leaves us floored,"
Lamented the Mouse.
"Never mind your superfluous gazes and take to the Pee Pee's edge,"
Said the Spokes-Goose.
"Look between the sun's glimmer upon the flow, as far as you peer,
Deep between glare and goose drivel, an answer you will dredge."

XV

The Spokes-Goose nodded to Pigweed for the flock to flee the bank,
And the trio stood alone to decipher the deep from the glare.
"I suppose, finding Lox in Ohio is an idea imported from elsewhere.
I just see frazzled mammals beside a Golem without hair."
So surmised the metaphysical Rabbit.
"Release your glower to push your skull's sockets through Sun's glitter,"

60

Advised Pearl.

"Perhaps the remedy rests with Rabbit and Mouse souls.
Friends! Spit East! Spit West! Spit North! Let's let go of all that is bitter

Book 4
Scene 3
Pearl's Riverbank Bimah

I

The trio watched the wads of spit float towards another state,
And Pearl felt that the Evil Eye was, once and for all, held at bay.
"Fred! Jarry! We have seen chickens as guiding, plumed glimmers.
We have seen the horrors of Shmuts and Geese in metaphysical sway."
So spoke the Golem, in plush baritone.
"What a night to have sailed the Santa Maria to this sacred stream,"
Preached Pearl from the riverbank.
"With her shattered hull, we can build something anew.
With port and stern, we can put together whatever you might dream."

II

Fred considered his dreams, both night and day,
And he listened to a sharp wind howl through dead cattails.
"My dreams always bring back Farzeenish! Old Monster Farzeenish!
Gnashing teeth! Tearing Mice! I am punished with a Farzeenish dream
tale!"
So cried the shaking Mouse.
"Oh Fred! Good Mouse! You've survived this dreamscape fully
unscathed,"
Replied Pearl.
"Here is, then, the plan, as we've neither bread nor Lox.
Cast off these pebbles into the currents; our fears and sins will be
bathed!"

III

All three swept up a handful of polished stones,
And Fred threw first, watching his pebbles sink.
"There, Fred! There stands proof of the lightness of your sins.
No rats flee your sinking stones as they settle by old marsh pink."
So encouraged the Golem.

"Do you now see your stones? Why, even your frown has strayed,"
Lectured Pearl.
"Under the flow, they have changed and hidden your monsters.
Dear Fred, you can now start anew, as your fears are washed away."

IV

Jarry swirled then studied the various stones in his paw
And he recognized the jagged pieces of crushed concrete.
"I hold in my paw what's left of an Empire never dreamed by Gibbons.
What secrets do these pieces hold dearly and discrete?"
So wondered the oddly well-read Rabbit.
"How far might a thieving rabbit toss his fears... his evil?"
Continued Jarry.
"Here is... oof! An old slab of a... oof! Building, into the brink.
This is my heaviest labor yet, such... huff! I grow Hercule... puff! regal."

V

Jarry heaved the largest concrete piece, causing a river wave,
And a Golem-sized water wall drenched the brooding bunny.
"I am soaked by the stream and yet, I remain ever so dry.
Now, somehow, I feel better... far less rash for my money."
So surmised the Hare.
"Say, Pearl. We've destroyed the very modern model of Saint Maria,"
Said Jarry.
"Suppose we salvage hull and port, build bold and stern
New worlds upon this shifting bar, this wild Pangaea."

VI

Pearl placed his ear upon the crushed facslmile
And sniffed for a welcomed spot to dig in his thumbs.
"One pull... OY... should do the... VEY... I hear a fracture!
Come, pull along with me! Don't sit on your bums."
So ordered the Golem.
"Ah, Pearl! Please take up all these divine planks!"
Pleaded Fred.

"Railings atop floorboards shall make my new cheese and seed bar.
There, I will serve sesame and rye, with cheese, to all Mice ranks."

VII

Pearl carried detached planks and railings to a scenic bank
And hammered in pegs for proper Mouse barstools.
"This seed palace should accompany a neighboring opera palace.
Here, Soprano Jo could sing to all the Mice of baritones quite cruel."
So dreamed the Mouse.
"For a dessert finale, Soprano Jo performs her wind-up doll, in French,"
Plotted Fred.
"She'll wind up her highest notes, to make all Mice giggle and swoon.
Then, from our pegs, we speak of our favorite baseball star, Johnny
Mensch."

VIII

Pearl laughed, while carrying the crow's nest to an intimate location,
And hid the remains of the spirit topmast in piles of dead leaves.
"Perfect, Pearl, location to open 'Jacque's Nest for Wayward Bunnies,'
A humble house for survivors of catastrophe, rabbits that grieve."
So said the Hare.
"Through these blades of grass, we'll sing of the 'Rabbit Electric',"
Fancied the poetry loving Jarry.
"From the splinters of conquest, I shall offer shelter to the dispossessed.
We'll sooth all wounds, accept the eccentric, the deeply eclectic."

IX

Jarry disappeared into his new office, for immediate business,
And Fred dusted off pegs for customers, keeping an eye for Soprano Jo.
"Pearl, can you see me through these damp leaves and supportive twigs?
These days of strife require Jacque's Nest hidden, a private chateau."
So queried the Hare.
"Pearl! Should Soprano Jo arrive, let her know of a concert at eight,"
Said Fred.
"We'll order quarts…no, pints…. No, gallons of seeds for the party.
I've not a clue how to get that many seeds, so diners will have to wait."

X

Fred, as well as Jarry, gleefully tended to their new businesses,
And Pearl noticed his feet starting to blend into the sandbar.
"Earth calls her son back home, without any Rabbi's consent.
There go my clay toes, my clay feet; I flake off a river lodestar."
So lamented the Golem.
"My flesh to secrete the river worms, river clams,"
Cried Pearl.
"To my crusted knees I dissolve, but still hear Pigweed about,
With such, I shall never again take the world as mere sham."

XI

Pearl melted up to his waist into the Scioto mud,
And red maple leaves covered his shoulders like epaulettes.
"I will finally refuse Leo the Inhaler, his anger, his consumption.
But see the Here! Mouse and Hare, I embraced a rightful Golem epitaph."
So smiled the one-time street beast.
"Away goes my chest, along with its Golem's heart,"
Said Pearl
"How is it that so many fail to know? How can it be
That Golems stand as nothing but beating…"

XII

Pearl's nose fell from his decayed ear, bouncing into the Scioto,
And the beloved proboscis bobbed east as a wind rose.
"There goes, before the grace of God, my fears and sins.
There, within nasal caverns, flow precious waters into my nose."
So choked out the remaining pieces of Monster.
"I hear melody blaring, the Rabbi's favorite Joplin tune,"
Mused Pearl.
"First chickens, then geese, now God has spoken, 'ice cream.'
I am seeing eye to eye with a reddish crayfish, napping on a dune."

XIV

With only Pearl's head above the Earth, a junco landed atop the Golem,
And the dark-eyed songstress began an aria, accompanied by snow.
"Ah! The Everlasting Light's finally upon me, oh dear sandy Bimah.
I've one prayer to sing, with head covered, before I sink too low."
So said the disappearing Faithful.
"Can it be that she has finally arrived, my dear Soprano Jo?"
Said Fred, at the edge of his opera palace.
"Prepare for her entrance! Prepare for her entrance!
What shall we say when she enters? What to say to Jo?"

XV

Only Pearl's eyes and mouth reached above the sand's surface,
And here he uttered his last words before disappearing.
"Dear pincer fish, do you devour the fetid of the Here?
Crawl to me and make me your new home, for your hiding."
So said what is now Earth.
"A truck wails out of season... Feel! Feel! Ice droplet,"
Whispered Pearl.
"In the shadow of a November freeze...
Can a Golem at long last desire chocolate?"

Biography

Les Epstein is a poet, playwright, opera librettist and educator. His work has appeared in journals in the United States, Philippines, India and the U.K., including Slant, The Bacopa Review, Mojave River Review, Clinch Mountain Review, and Jelly Bucket, as well as the anthologies Heat the Grease (Gnashing Teeth Publishing) and Pain & Renewal (Vita Brevis Press). His work was honored by the Writers Guild of Gainesville (FL) in 2021 and has been featured in the podcast, "Sunflower Sutras," broadcast out of Washburn University. His chapbook, "Kip Divided," will appear, from Finishing Line Press, in 2022. As a playwright, his work has been staged by such theaters as the Belfast Maskers (Maine), Greenbrier Valley Theater (WV), Stone's Throw Dinner Theater (Missouri) and the Roy Arias Studio (New York). He contributed libretti for two operas, Barefoot (1997 premiere) and Miss Lucy (2011 premiere). Cyberwit released a collection of his short plays and libretti (Seven) in 2018. Epstein's bi-lingual collaboration with Claudia de Franko, Llorona of the River is available through Silver Birchington Plays. He received undergraduate degrees in Theater Performance and English from Otterbein College, and MA in English from Miami (Ohio) University and continued with studies in Literature at New York University and in Theater Education at The Ohio State University. He completed his teacher training at Mary Baldwin College. In addition to work with theater, opera and ballet companies, from North Carolina to New York City, he spent ten seasons as Education Director and Production Coordinator for Opera/Columbus and another seven as Executive Director for the Children's Theater of Winston-Salem, before settling in as a teacher with Community High School (Roanoke) for which he has staged more than thirty-five productions.

Other Volumes from Gnashing Teeth Publishing

Heat the Grease, We're Frying Up Some Poetry anthology

Love Notes You'll Never Read anthology

Winter limited release zine

Rain Minnows [Notecards and Poems] by Joshua Bridgwater Hamilton

Insurrection anthology

SHE: Seen. Heard. Engaged. Vol. 1 youth anthology

Meditations & Mediations by Dr. Rebecah Hall

places I never want to see again by Keriann Gilson

Forthcoming Books

Lunafly by Raymond Luczak

La Santa Madre Tamalera by Juan Manuel Perez

Adrift by Joanna Grant

Ghostword by Crisosto Apache

Pandemic Zoom by Tom Murphy

1st Quarter Preventable Gun Violence. 2021. Vol. 1 anthology

You can purchase our books at http://gnashingteethpublishing.com

www.ingramcontent.com/pod-product-compliance
Lightning Source LLC
Chambersburg PA
CBHW070814260626
47161CB00006B/2274